S0-BUD-514

TO JIMMY

# THE BOY

# WHO CRIED WOLF

RETOLD BY KATHERINE EVANS

*Illustrated by the Author*

ALBERT WHITMAN & COMPANY • CHICAGO

Published simultaneously in the Dominion of Canada by
George J. McLeod Ltd., Toronto    Lithographed in the U.S.A.
© Copyright 1960 By Albert Whitman & Co.
Standard Book Number 8075-0863-2    L.C. Card 60-8429
Third Printing, 1970

SELAH, WASHINGTON
7965

LINCE LIBRARY    TITLE 2 ESEA

There was once a young boy named Peter.
He lived with his grandfather,
a poor shepherd, who was growing very old.

All they owned in the world
was a flock of sheep,
which the old shepherd prized highly.

The time came when the grandfather
could no longer take the sheep
to the green meadow on the hill.

One day, he said to Peter,
"My grandson, you have grown
to be a fine, big boy.
It is time for you to take the sheep
to the meadow. My legs are old and stiff."

Peter did not want to leave
his playmates in the village.
But his grandfather
had always been very kind to him.
So he said, "I will gladly take the sheep
to the meadow, Grandfather."

"Watch them carefully,"
said the grandfather.
"They are all we own in the world."

Peter took the flock of fat, white sheep
to the beautiful green meadow on the hill.
Here, he sat under an olive tree,
and guarded his flock
while they grazed on the hillside.

He looked down into the village.
He saw the villagers
going about their daily tasks.
He saw the farmer hoeing his cabbages.
The farmer's sons were racing
with their dog.

Peter watched some boys
fishing from the river bank.

He <u>heard</u> the milkmaid singing
as she <u>carried</u> her pail of milk
to <u>market</u>.

<u>Peter</u> said to himself,
"How lonely it is <u>here</u>,
so high and <u>far</u> away <u>from</u> <u>everyone</u>."

Then one day, he had an idea.
As soon as the sheep
had <u>started</u> to graze on the hillside,
Peter <u>ran</u> down the hill and called:
"A wolf!  A wolf!"

The <u>villagers</u> left t<u>heir</u> tasks
and <u>ran</u> to the hill.
The <u>farmer</u> stopped his <u>work and ran.</u>
His sons and <u>their</u> dog <u>ran</u> after him.

The boys who <u>were</u> fishing in the <u>river</u>
<u>ran as</u> fast as they could,
waving their fishing poles.

The milkmaid with <u>her</u> pail of milk
<u>ran</u> up the hill.

When they <u>reached</u> the top,
they <u>were</u> all out of <u>breath.</u>
But instead of finding a wolf,
they found <u>Peter</u>
lying under the olive tree.

He laughed and laughed.
"It's all a joke," he said.

They were all happy that there was no wolf.
But they were very unhappy
about running so hard and so fast for nothing.

Peter felt <u>lonelier</u> than <u>before</u>.
A day<u>s later</u> he thought,
"I'll try it again.
What fun to have <u>everyone</u>
come <u>running</u>."
He put his hands to his mouth
and called as loud as he could:
"Help, help, a wolf! A wolf!"

Again the villagers left their tasks.
Again the farmer stopped his work.
He and his sons,
and the boys fishing by the river,
and the milkmaid
all grabbed sticks and ran to help.

This time,
when they found the sheep grazing,
and Peter rolling on the grass laughing,
they were very angry.

One day, not long <u>afterwards,</u>
<u>Peter</u> was sitting alone
<u>under</u> the olive tree.

Looking around him,
he saw a big <u>gray</u> wolf.
Sly and wicked it was,
<u>crouching</u> behind the bushes
at the top of the hill.

SELAH, WASHINGTON

TITLE 2 ESEA    7965

The wolf's eyes gleamed
as it watched the fat sheep,
and its long <u>red</u> tongue
hung out of its mouth.

Peter was so frightened
that he could hear his heart
beat louder and faster.

He jumped up
and shouted to the villagers:
"A wolf!  A wolf!"

But everyone in the village said:
"That <u>Peter</u>! He's calling wolf again.
This time, we will pay no attention to him."

The farmer did not stop hoeing his cabbages.
His sons went on playing with their dog.
The boys sat on the river bank fishing.
The milkmaid did not stop her singing.

Poor Peter called and called again.
He <u>tried</u> to <u>frighten</u> the wolf away.
But the wolf was not <u>afraid</u> of one small boy.

LINCE LIBRARY

The wolf <u>sprang</u> <u>from</u> the bushes
and killed most of the boy's flock.
The <u>rest</u> of the sheep <u>ran</u> away
and <u>were</u> <u>never</u> seen again.

When people in the village <u>heard</u>
that this time
there <u>really</u> had been a wolf,
they shook <u>their</u> heads and said:

"A <u>liar</u> will not be believed,
even when he speaks the <u>truth</u>."

7965

7965

**398.24**
E∨
**EVANS, KATHERINE**
The boy who cried wolf

| DATE DUE | | | |
|---|---|---|---|
| 12 | | | |
| OCT 22 1973 | | | |
| OCT 30 '75 | FEB 18 1980 | | |
| FEB 13 '76 | MAR 4 1980 | | |
| OCT 7 78 | | | |
| DEC 13 '78 | | | |
| MAR 15 78 | | | |
| JAN 18 '79 | | | |
| MAR 20 '79 | | | |
| OCT 1 1979 | | | ALESCO |

JOHN CAMPBELL SCHOOL LIBRARY
SELAH, WASHINGTON

TITLE 2 ESEA